McDUFF STORIES

This book belongs to:

_____

In Memoriam:

McIvor, Lucy, Snow

First Edition
1 3 5 7 9 10 8 6 4 2

This book is set in Cochin.
Reinforced binding

ISBN 0-7868-1930-8
Library of Congress Cataloging-in-Publication Data on file.

Visit www.hyperionbooksforchildren.com

McDUFF'S
WILD ROMP

ROSEMARY WELLS • SUSAN JEFFERS

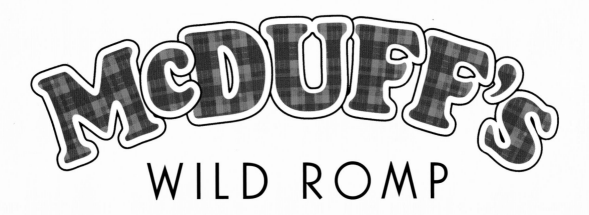

HYPERION BOOKS FOR CHILDREN
NEW YORK

McDuff found a warm, sunny spot under the baby's swing, where the baby's Turkey Tidbits fell.

He was just going into a Turkey Tidbit trance when suddenly Lucy called. "Come, McDuff! It's Sunday dinner time!"

McDuff knew they were not heading for Lake Ocarina,
or the Take-Out Steak-Out, or Dog Training School.

He knew they were going to Aunt Frieda's house.

During Sunday dinner, McDuff was supposed to stay in the parlor with Purlina. Purlina would not let McDuff sit in the chair. She clicked her teeth at him. Purlina would not let him sit under the chair. She showed her claws.

Purlina would not let McDuff stretch out on the heating vent.
She spat at him.

Purlina did not want him behind Uncle Nate.
She flattened her ears and hissed like a log sizzling in the fire.
"What was that?" asked Uncle Nate.

The noise startled Aunt Frieda. She bumped into Grandpa Floyd, who stepped on Cousin Rose's foot, who knocked against the baby's high chair.

A Turkey Tidbit fell to the floor. It rolled under the dining room table.

Nobody saw it but McDuff and Purlina.

McDuff began to creep under the dining room table. Purlina began to creep in from the parlor.

They slunk toward the Turkey Tidbit while the family ate their crab cakes. Salad followed the crab cakes. Closer and closer they tiptoed.

They sneaked and peeked under the table.

Just as the family was finishing the salad, McDuff and Purlina
reached the Turkey Tidbit.

There was a hullabaloo right under the dining room table.
Fred jumped to his feet and knocked over his chair.

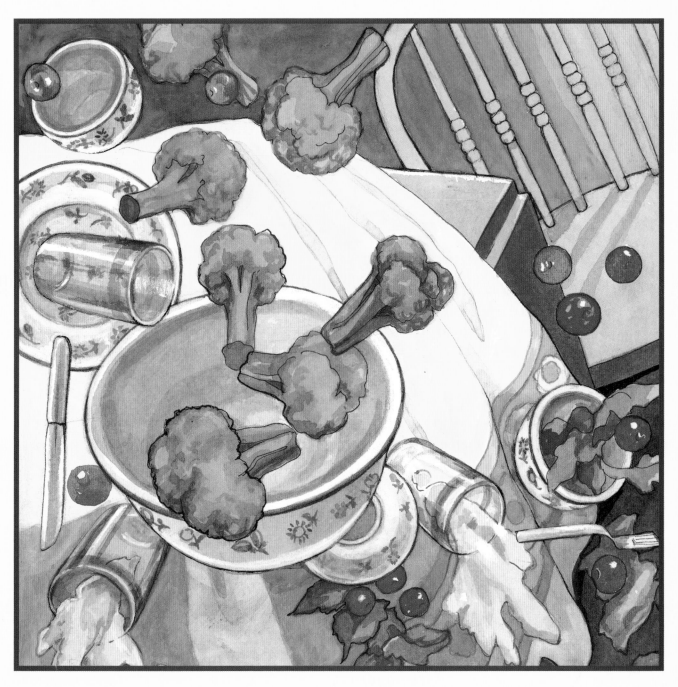

"Stop, McDuff!" commanded Fred.
"Bad pussycat!" shouted Aunt Frieda.

Up the stairs and down the stairs, Purlina chased McDuff.
But she did not catch him before McDuff had swallowed the
Turkey Tidbit whole.

Purlina rolled McDuff off the sofa and across the carpet.
But the Turkey Tidbit was gone forever.

"What got into you, McDuff?" asked Fred.

"We are embarrassed, McDuff!" cried Lucy.

The parlor furniture had to be put back on its feet.
The lamps had to be plugged in again and the carpet vacuumed.

"Whatever could have happened to make a quiet, gentle dog and cat behave like wild tigers and bears?" asked Uncle Nate.

Nobody could answer that question — not Aunt Frieda, Cousin Rose, Grandpa Floyd, or Lucy, or Fred.
Aunt Frieda served coffee and her seven-layer chocolate dream cake.

The baby liked the seven-layer chocolate dream cake much better than the Turkey Tidbits.
So she took the last of the Turkey Tidbits and threw it on the floor.

"Again!" said the baby.

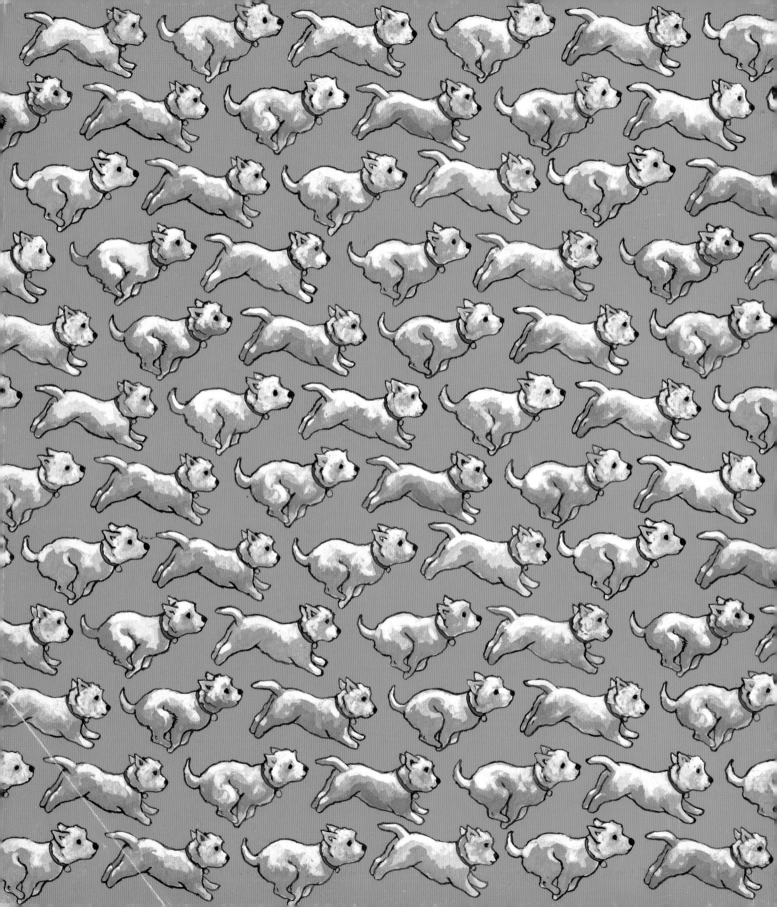